Puffi

# HALF HEROES

The Crocs have won the chance to play at half-time during the AFL Grand Final. It doesn't get any better than this.

But their old enemy Cactus is back. He's greener and meaner than ever and he's out to destroy football for good.

Can Nick, Ella and Bruiser win the game and save everyone in the MCG?

## read all the books in the series...

1. THE CURSED CUP
2. FORWARD LINE FREAK
3. BUGS FROM BEYOND
4. OUTBREAK ON THE OVAL
5. FOOTYBOT FACE-OFF
6. THE FANGED FOOTYS
7. T-REX AT TRAINING
8. HALF-TIME HEROES

# Crawf's Kick it to Nick: Half-Time Heroes

**Shane Crawford & Adrian Beck**

Puffin Books

For three huge Hawk fans, Jane, Olivia and Clara.
We make a great team – AB

For my four boys, Charlie, Ben, Jack and Harry.
Thanks for keeping me a kid at heart! – SC

PUFFIN BOOKS

UK | USA | Canada | Ireland | Australia
India | New Zealand | South Africa | China

Penguin Books is part of the Penguin Random House group of companies whose addresses can be found at global.penguinrandomhouse.com.

Penguin Random House Australia

First published by Penguin Books Australia Ltd, 2015

1 3 5 7 9 10 8 6 4 2

Text copyright © Shane Crawford and Adrian Beck, 2015
Illustrations copyright © Heath McKenzie, 2015

The moral right of the authors and the illustrator has been asserted.

All rights reserved. Without limiting the rights under copyright reserved above, no part of this publication may be reproduced, stored in or introduced into a retrieval system, or transmitted, in any form or by any means (electronic, mechanical, photo-copying, recording or otherwise), without the prior written permission of both the copyright owner and the above publisher of this book.

Cover and text design by Bruno Herfst © Penguin Group (Australia)
Photographs by Wayne McPherson
Typeset in 15pt ITC Officina Sans
Colour separation by Splitting Image Colour Studio, Clayton, Victoria
Printed and bound in Australia by Griffin Press, an accredited ISO AS/NZS 14001 Environmental Management Systems printer.

National Library of Australia Cataloguing-in-Publication data available.

ISBN: 978 0 14 330792 1

puffin.com.au

®™ THE AFL LOGO AND COMPETING TEAM LOGOS, EMBLEMS AND NAMES ON THIS PRODUCT ARE ALL TRADE MARKS OF AND USED UNDER LICENCE FROM THE OWNER THE AUSTRALIAN FOOTBALL LEAGUE BY WHOM ALL © COPYRIGHT AND OTHER RIGHTS OF REPRODUCTION ARE RESERVED.

MIX
Paper from responsible sources
FSC® C009448

# A NOTE FROM CRAWF...

**It's the Grand Final and the Crocs are right amongst the action!**

Every AFL season ends with a bang on that one day in September at the mighty MCG. Personally, I played in just one Grand Final. It took 17 years and over 300 games to get there, but it was worth it when we won. In my heart I knew going into the game that it'd be my last. My knees were shot. So I tried to enjoy every moment of what I secretly knew was the very end of my career. I even smuggled my son Charlie into the ute with me during the Grand Final Parade!

It was a truly incredible feeling when the final siren sounded. Not even taking home the Brownlow compared. It felt like living a dream – which, in a way, it was. This is how I see it: winning a game is the reason you play footy. But experiencing that feeling with your teammates is the reason you *love* footy.

Nick and his friends will get to taste some Grand Final action in this edition of Kick it to Nick. Let's hope it's not spoilt for them when an old enemy returns!

## THE STORY SO FAR...

Nick, Bruiser and Ella are three footy-mad students who play for the Cobar Creek Crocs Under Elevens.

It's been a rollercoaster season for the Crocs. Nick and his friends have had to deal with some full-on freaky challenges, including an attack from a molten-metal monster, a bizarre weed creature, mutant bugs and their ferocious queen, malfunctioning football-playing robots, footys that grow fangs and a terrifying T-rex!

And now Nick's discovered what's been causing all the deadly danger on the oval: purple goop from outer space! He has the substance trapped inside a footy, and plans to dispose of it once and for all. Then he'll be free to enjoy all the highlights of Grand Final Week.

At least that's the plan...

# Chapter 1

**Ten seconds.**

That was about how long Bruiser's fringe stayed slicked back.

The big guy was in a suit. And Nick was in a suit. And Ella was in a suit.

They'd bought their outfits from a charity store to get into the spirit of Brownlow night. Ella's AFL-star dad — Wally 'Marz' Marwin — was a chance to win the medal, and because it was school holidays they were allowed to stay up late to watch the whole broadcast at Nick's place.

But Nick was beginning to wonder if this had been such a good idea. It was super exciting, but it was also fully nerve-wracking.

Ella had been pacing the lounge room since the votes had been announced for Round 3. Two hours ago.

Finally, the AFL boss was finishing Round 18: 'W...Marwin. Three votes!'

'Yeah!' cried Ella, jumping up on the coffee table as Marz hit the lead. 'That's what I'm talkin' about!'

'Hey,' said Nick. 'That's my line.'

'I reckon Marz can do it,' said Bruiser. 'He got thirty-nine touches in the last round. Mind you, Joel Selwood only got one vote in a 2014 match for the same thing.'

On telly, Marz was all suited up, sitting beside Ella's mum. The TV host promised they'd announce the votes for the final rounds...right after the break!

Ella hurled a packet of chips at the TV.

Nick had always dreamt about winning the Brownlow. If it came down to choosing between winning a premiership or a Brownlow, Nick would be tempted to go for the individual honour of hearing his name called out on football's night of nights.

'Nicholas Darrel Harvey,' yelled Nick's mum from the hallway. 'I cannot believe what I just found under your bed.'

Under my bed? Nick thought. He swallowed. Had his mum found the footy that he'd injected with glowing purple space goop? Space goop that had the power to cause big-time freakiness.

'Out here right now, young man!'

Nick slowly got to his feet. He hadn't known what to do with the footy. How exactly do you get rid of dangerous intergalactic goop? Does it go in the normal bin or the recycling?

'Anything to say for yourself?' asked Nick's mum, holding something behind her back.

'Um, you really shouldn't be touching that,' said Nick. 'It's probably some kind of toxic waste.'

'I'll say,' said Nick's mum, revealing Nick's lunch box.

She opened it. The stench of a mouldy sandwich and a week-old banana hit Nick.

He staggered back.

'How long has this been under your bed?'

'Gross,' said Nick. 'Sorry, Mum.'

'This will need to be scrubbed clean, young man. You're lucky your friends are here, otherwise I'd make you do it right now,' she said. 'Oh, and where did you get that purple night-light footy that's under your bed?'

'Um,' said Nick. 'I...found it.'

'It looks faulty. Possibly dangerous. I'd ditch it, mister.'

'Good call.'

'Right. Now try to keep Ella calm till the Brownlow is over, okay?'

Nick glanced back into the lounge room. Ella was hiding behind the couch.

'No worries,' he lied.

Nick slurped on his apple juice as he sat back on the couch.

'Shhhhh!' said Ella over Nick's shoulder.

The leaderboard showed Marz had dropped two votes behind. It was the middle of the last round. Only a Best on Ground would win it from here.

'What do you reckon?' whispered Nick to Bruiser. 'You're the stats genius. Can he get the three points?'

'It's doable, but you never know with umps.'

Ella popped up behind them. 'If you two don't shut up I'll knock your heads together.'

'N...Fyfe. One vote.' The AFL boss began announcing the votes for Marz's game.

'Why does he do the big pause before the surname?' muttered Ella.

'M...Barlow. Two votes.'

'Here we go. Here we go,' said Ella.

'W...' announced the AFL boss.

The cameras cut to Marz's table. Ella's mum looked nervous. Marz and his teammates were listening intently.

'Spit! It! Out!' yelled Ella.

'...Minson. Three votes.'

On telly, Marz clapped graciously as the winner was announced.

In Nick's lounge room, Ella popped two packets of chips, kicked over the magazine rack, then dumped the popcorn bowl over her head.

She stood dead still, letting the kernels tumble down her body.

'Um. Bad luck, Ella,' said Nick.

'So close,' said Bruiser, leaning cautiously away from her.

Then Nick's big brother, Lucas, strode into the room. He ignored the bowl on Ella's head and sat on the coffee table in front of Nick. He flicked the channel.

'Hey! We were watching that,' said Nick.

'Cool it, butt brain,' said Lucas. 'I'll be, like, two seconds, max.'

He'd changed it to a sports panel show. The host was mid-sentence. 'And check out this young gun.'

A photo of Nick kicking a goal came up on screen.

'Um, why are you on TV?' asked Bruiser.

'No idea,' said Nick. 'Isn't that our winning goal against the Eels?'

Lucas shrugged. 'Quiet!' he said.

'The Harvster can sure work the camera,' said Nick, pointing to himself.

Ella tilted up the bowl so she could see properly. 'You look constipated.'

'This killer shot is the winner of our sports photography competition,' said the TV host. 'So, well done to young photographer Lucas Harvey!'

Lucas went red.

'Wow,' said Nick. 'Nice one!'

'Lucas has won the opportunity to take photos at Saturday's AFL Grand Final. But that's not all,' the TV host continued. 'Thanks to Lucas, the team in this photo are winners as well. The Cobar Creek Crocs will be playing a half-time exhibition match at the AFL Grand Final.'

What?

Nick dropped his juice. It spilt all over his suit pants, but he barely noticed.

# Chapter 2

**It didn't seem real. The Crocs were** going to play at the MCG on Grand Final Day. This was massive. Although Lucas hadn't looked thrilled with his prize.

'I thought I'd win a thousand bucks or a new camera or something,' he said.

The Crocs' coach, Mr Baxter, had rung around to tell the team, and organised a training session for the next day.

In the morning, about an hour before

training, Nick retrieved the footy filled with space goop from under his bed. The ball was glowing purple. Brighter than ever.

The supernatural disasters on the oval had all been caused by this substance. The only thing left for Nick to do was destroy it to keep everyone safe. But how?

There was a knock on the front door.

'Coming!' He stepped into the hallway and opened it.

'Have you seen yourself in those PJs?' asked Ella, laughing and pointing at Nick's pyjamas. They had heart patterns with *Mummy's Special Boy* written on them.

Nick crossed his arms, hoping to cover some of the love hearts. He changed the subject. 'Aren't you a bit early?'

Ella had her Crocs gear on. 'I can't wait

for training. Let's grab Bruiser and head to the oval for some kick-to-kick.'

'Um, I'm kinda in the middle of something,' said Nick, glancing back at his room.

Ella looked past him. 'Woah. Is that it? Is that the freaky footy?'

Nick nodded.

She walked in and knelt beside the glowing ball.

'I thought you said you'd destroyed it.'

'No, I said I was *going to* destroy it. I just haven't figured out how.'

Ella shook her head. 'I don't need to tell you how dangerous it is.'

'No — you don't.'

'I can hear it fizzing like lemonade or something.'

'I wouldn't try to drink it.' Nick zipped up the ball in his sports bag. 'Give me a sec to change and we'll get going. We can work out a way to get rid of it after training.'

'I can't believe we're going to play at the MCG,' said Ella.

'I'm not sure who's more pumped,' said Bruiser. 'Me or my dad!'

'With the footy world watching, I might be drafted on the spot,' said Nick.

As they walked through the four-square courts, Bruiser booted his footy down to the oval and ran after it.

'Isn't it nice to know that all the freakiness has been sucked out of the oval?' said Ella.

'Yeah, but it's a pity that all the freakiness is now inside this bag that I'm carrying,' muttered Nick.

This season they had faced a molten metal monster, mutant bugs, a team of malfunctioning robots, fanged footys, and a rampaging re-animated dinosaur skeleton. Plus, one of their schoolmates, Kyle 'Cactus' Cassidy, had even turned into a mutant weed creature. And Nick had almost turned into one too.

Nick wondered how Cactus was. No one had heard from him since. But his mum owned a huge research company called Cassidy Corp. Hopefully they'd been able to help him.

Nick dropped his bag on the creek-side wing, further away from everyone else's stuff. Then he ran onto the field.

It was their best training session yet. Everyone was buzzing.

Nick imagined the oval's lights and grandstand were the light towers and Great Southern Stand of the MCG. He pictured himself taking a game-saving mark, like Brendon Goddard's screamer in the dying minutes of the 2010 Grand Final.

To Ella's disgust, Nick even practised his celebrations for the TV close-ups.

After a warm-down, Mr Baxter addressed the team. 'Righto, Crocs, let's get something straight. Saturday's game is just like any other match.'

'Yeah, sure. Just like any other match in front of one hundred thousand fans,' said Reevers.

'Don't try to be flashy out there, Crocs.

We want another good, honest team effort — that's what works for us.'

Ella stared at Nick. 'Are you listening?' she whispered. 'No look-at-me strutting. No unnecessary one-hander marks, and definitely no handstand celebrations.'

Nick pretended not to hear her.

'And one last thing,' said Mr Baxter. 'Our season was officially over when we bowed out to the Dingos, so we need to vote on a new captain.'

'What?' said Taylor.

'Huh?' Reevers seemed about to crack it.

Mr Baxter held up his hands to silence them. 'There's no reason why the current captain can't be voted back in.'

'Taylor for captain again, then,' said Reevers as pens and paper were passed around.

Kingy glared at everyone threateningly.

Nick glanced around at the team. He was pretty sure no one would want Taylor to be captain for another season. He was a bad sport and a ball hog, plus half the Crocs were scared of him and his mates, Reevers and Kingy.

Being stripped of the captaincy had been the worst moment of Nick's life. But now he was sure everyone would give him another go. He eagerly scrawled down his own name.

Mr Baxter collected the papers and added up the votes. 'Rightio, then.' He looked up at Taylor. 'Sorry, Taylor. Thanks for leading the Crocs this season.'

Taylor fumed.

'Re-count,' said Reevers.

'The next captain of the Crocs is...'

Mr Baxter paused. It went even longer than the pauses at the Brownlow.

'Hurry up!' said Jake.

'Just tell us,' said Nick. He couldn't wait to hear his name called out.

'All right, all right,' said Mr Baxter. 'The new Crocs captain is number seven – Ella Marwin.'

# Chapter 3

**'Huh?' said Nick.**

'Ye-oooouch!' cried Ella as Bruiser hugged her, spinning her around.

Nick watched the other Crocs closing in, all high fives and woohoos.

Ella was grinning from ear to ear.

'Congratulations, Ella,' said Mr Baxter. 'Top choice, Crocs.'

Nick shook Ella's hand. He didn't really know what to say. Neither did she.

'Great stuff,' he said finally. He knew he should feel happy for her, but there was a huge lump in his throat. 'Um, well done, Ella.'

'Hold your horses,' called the principal, Mr Blumfield, as he waddled down the slope. 'I ought to be the one to officially congratulate next year's captain.'

As he reached the wing, Mr Blumfield held out his hand for Taylor to shake.

'Uh-uh,' said Mr Baxter.

'Then who?'

Mr Baxter nodded at Ella.

'Oh, wonderful!' Mr Blumfield shook Ella's hand. 'Congratulations, Miss Marwin. Obviously, having a famous father has come in handy.'

The smile fell from Ella's face.

'Haven't you seen Ella play?' asked Jake. 'Her dad's got nothing to do with this.'

'Ella earned the captaincy herself,' agreed Ollie.

Mr Blumfield was going red in the face.

Bruiser nodded. 'Ella will be the next Abbey Holmes for sure,' he said, comparing Ella to the first woman to kick 100 goals in a season.

'Thanks, guys,' said Ella. 'Abbey's cool, but I won't stop till I'm giving Buddy

Franklin a run for his money.'

'I don't doubt that for second,' muttered Mr Blumfield, leaning forwards, his chin wobbling with every word. 'Now, pay attention, Crocs. Playing at the Grand Final is a huge honour. And if anyone's actions reflect badly on our school, well, there'll be hell to pay.'

The Crocs fell silent.

'Got it?'

They all jumped. Then a few nodded.

'Right. So do us proud on Saturday,' said Mr Blumfield.

The Crocs began packing up.

'Don't be late for the Grand Final Parade,' called Mr Baxter as Taylor, Reevers and Kingy stomped off up the slope. 'It won't wait for you.'

As Ella talked tactics with Mr Baxter,

Nick took Bruiser aside.

'Wasn't I the obvious choice for captain?' asked Nick. 'I mean, why *wouldn't* people vote for me?'

'I didn't,' said Bruiser. 'Sorry, Nick. You're one of our best players. So's Taylor. But Ella got my vote. She'll kill it.'

Nick shook his head. Even his best friend hadn't voted for him. He stormed over to his bag. His mood only got worse when he remembered the space goop footy inside.

He carefully picked up the bag. Then something scraped his neck.

It was only a twig, from one of the trees that lined the boundary. But Nick had the strangest feeling — the feeling that he was being watched.

'Hello?' There was no response. Just the

sound of rustling trees. 'Anyone there?'

Weird.

Nick racked his brains for how to get rid of the footy. Could he burn it? Unfortunately, the only fireplace he had access to was the woodfired pizza oven in Ella's backyard. And there was no way he was going to ask her for help. Not now.

He wondered if Bruiser had any ideas — he was the brainiac after all. But as Nick looked over at the big fella high-fiving Ella, he decided he'd figure it out himself.

'How am I gunna get rid of you?' Nick asked the bag. Then he noticed the zipper wasn't done up the whole way. And there wasn't a purple glow shining through the opening.

Nick opened the bag.

The space goop footy was missing!

## Chapter 4

**The next morning, Nick was still** freaking out.

The space goop must have been stolen, but who had taken it? And why? Who even knew about it apart from Nick, Ella and Bruiser?

Then it hit him. Mrs Cassidy had known, and she was the boss of Cassidy Corp. Probably her scientists knew too. Could she have ordered them to track it down to study it? He needed to find her.

Over breakfast, Nick googled Cassidy Corp. Mrs Cassidy was announcing a sponsorship deal for one of the Grand Final teams at their open training session. He figured this might be his only chance to confront her.

Nick's mum had already left for work. Lucas was supposed to be in charge, but he'd gone to a friend's house. Typical.

The training session was at an oval out in the suburbs. Nick knew his mum wouldn't want him going on his own, but this was an emergency...

As soon as he stepped off the bus, he was surrounded by fans all proudly wearing their team's colours.

It was incredible. There were 10,000 people at the ground, singing their song over and over. Nick knew it was a great Grand Final Week tradition, but he'd never been to an open training session before.

The crowd erupted when the players hit the ground. These footy superstars were close enough to touch!

It was hard not to get caught up in the excitement. If Nick wasn't on such a serious mission he might even have had his face painted.

There was a stage set up between the grandstands. Nick figured that had to be where Mrs Cassidy would be appearing.

Nick pushed through the crowd. A woman was standing at the backstage entrance with a list of names.

'Hi,' said Nick. He flashed his most innocent smile. 'I'm just here for the Cassidy Corp announcement.'

The woman put her arm in his way. 'Really? And your name is?'

'Um, Smith.'

'Smith?'

'Yeah. First name, ahhh, Norm,' said Nick.

The woman produced a walkie-talkie. 'Security.'

Then Nick spotted Mrs Cassidy only a few metres away, walking with two big men in suits. She was still limping from her encounter with the T-rex.

'Mrs Cassidy!' called Nick.

'You!' she replied, wide-eyed. She motioned for the woman to let Nick through. 'Please tell me a stegosaurus isn't lurking around here somewhere.'

'No way,' said Nick, then he thought about it. 'Well, who knows. Anyway, listen, sorry to ask this, but you know that strange purple goop we found on the oval? Well, you haven't, y'know, stolen it, have you?'

'Stolen it?' But then Mrs Cassidy began to look impressed. 'So you managed to retrieve the substance, did you? Clever boy. No wonder my clean-up team found no trace of it.'

'Um, I *did* have it. But now it's sort of been stolen.'

'Well, you'd better work out who has it, quick smart,' said Mrs Cassidy. 'The tests I did that day clearly showed the substance has all sorts of strange capabilities.'

'Like?'

'Well...' Mrs Cassidy looked at Nick. 'You might know more about it than I do. How do you think the substance might affect things?'

Nick considered every threat he had faced this season.

'Metal could come alive,' he said. 'Plants and animals could mutate. Machines could start thinking for themselves. Fossils could come back to life...'

'Dear me,' said Mrs Cassidy. 'It also seemed to me that the substance was becoming unstable. I suspect it might erupt, and when it does my guess is that it's likely to warp everything it touches.'

'What? You mean all those crazy effects, all at once?'

Mrs Cassidy nodded sternly.

She was called away, but as she left she mouthed the words 'find it'.

On Friday, the city was packed for the Grand Final Parade. There were skills comps, media broadcasts and bands playing footy songs. You could even listen to footy stories being read aloud at Fed Square. It was pretty much footy heaven. And, this year, the Crocs were part of it.

Nick waited with all the other parade participants near the Arts Centre on St Kilda Road.

He was standing side by side with the best AFL players in the country. Even though he was still stressing about finding the space goop footy, that didn't stop him from collecting as many signatures as possible. Eventually, Mr Baxter had to send him away.

The Crocs were put in pairs to ride in the backs of cars at the front of the parade. Nick was with Taylor. At least he'd avoided Ella and Bruiser. They were in the car ahead. He hadn't talked to either of them for two days.

A marching band led them off. It was playing the Crocs' song! The crowd clapped in time.

Nick waved as they crawled along. Plenty of people waved back. He could certainly get used to this sort of thing.

'Mate, look at those guys,' muttered Taylor.

Mate? Were they back to being friends now that neither of them was captain?

'They're waving, but they've got no idea who we are. How lame!'

'They're just excited,' said Nick, wondering how he and Taylor had ever been mates in the first place.

As the cars began crossing Princes Bridge towards the city, Nick noticed Marz up ahead doing a TV interview.

Marz pointed out Ella as her car

approached. 'Make sure you get a shot of my daughter,' he yelled to the cameraman proudly.

Then it was all camera flashes.

Ella was shaking her head, looking unimpressed. Nick knew she hated getting media attention just because she had a famous dad.

Nick turned and stared down the Yarra River at the MCG. His heart beat faster at the sight of it. This was the home of Aussie sport. A place where heroes were made. And where he would be playing in just 24 hours.

Then something green caught Nick's eye. It was a boy with a spiky green hairdo, standing on the bridge railing. He looked familiar.

He lifted his head.

It was Cactus. And he was staring straight at Nick.

'Huh?' said Nick. Why was Cactus here? Had Mrs Cassidy managed to cure his nasty habit of morphing into a weed creature?

Nick waved nervously, and looked around to see if anyone else had noticed Cactus. But everyone was focussed on the commotion caused by Ella and Marz ahead.

Then Nick realised that Cactus wasn't standing on the bridge rail at all. He was being supported by a branch growing out of a tree down on the riverbank.

More branches were swaying behind him.

Cactus was controlling them all.

'Hey, Nick, you big footy star,' cried Cactus. 'You might think the Crocs are the centre of attention now, but just you wait till tomorrow...'

*Pop! Pop! Pop!*

Nick jumped as a bunch of balloons burst — all stabbed by tiny claw-like branches.

'It's sure to go off with a bang!' cried Cactus as he dropped out of view.

Nick undid his seatbelt and stood to peer over the Yarra. He spotted Cactus using a branch to lower himself into the window of a passing river taxi.

Cactus was free. He was definitely not cured. And he really seemed to be holding a grudge.

What the heck was he planning?

# Chapter 5

**The school minibus arrived at Nick's** house at 10.30am the next day. Lucas was already on board as Nick hurried through his front yard, shoving gear into his bag. His mum gave him a big hug and a kiss as he stepped onto the bus. But Nick was too excited to get embarrassed.

Mr Morris waved at Nick. He was busy discussing tactics with Mr Baxter who was driving. Nick was pleased their current coach had invited him along. In the next row, Mr Blumfield was busy talking to a man in an AFL polo top.

There was only one spot left for Nick — between Ella and Bruiser. It was just like the day he'd become captain at the start of the season.

'Park yourself, Nick,' said Mr Baxter. 'Righto, Crocs, next stop the Grand Final!'

Nick squeezed miserably into the seat.

'Hey,' said Bruiser.

'Hey,' said Nick.

Ella kept staring out the window.

There was silence for a few minutes.

'So, um, Cactus is on the loose,' said Nick quietly. 'And he's still controlling trees and stuff.'

'What?' said Ella.

The AFL rep got to his feet. 'Okay, team

captain, Ella Marwin? Raise your hand, please. We'd love a photo of you for social media.'

Ella raised her hand. Nick looked away. 'Smile!'

Nick kept to himself for the rest of the trip. He watched the Grand Final Day excitement building in the streets. Supporters were everywhere, showing their colours. Shops and cafes were decorated with balloons and scarves. Grand Final flags lined the streets and planes flew overhead in formation.

It was always the best day of the year, but this time it didn't feel that way to Nick — not with a missing space goop footy, an old enemy on the loose and everyone making a fuss of the new Crocs' captain.

But as the bus entered the MCG from

the south side, Nick's spirits started to lift. This must be where the AFL players come in, thought Nick. He felt honoured to be treated the same way.

They parked inside the stadium, right next to the bus spaces reserved for the Grand Final teams.

Nick was last off.

Following everyone else, Nick passed an entrance that led up to the oval. Suddenly it felt real. They were totally about to play at the MCG! This place had hosted the Olympics and Commonwealth Games, it was the scene of Warnie's 700th wicket and it'd delivered countless footy highlights...And now the Crocs were playing here!

After ditching their gear, they were shown to their seats in the Members'

Stand. They had a killer view of the fireworks, rock bands and the Premiership Cup arriving via hot air balloon.

Mr Morris sat down in the empty seat beside Nick and scuffed his hair.

'I'm so proud of you all!' he said, his moustache wiggling. 'This is awfully exciting!'

'You can't tell me this isn't awesome,' Nick said to Lucas. 'I'll never understand what you've got against footy.'

'Nothing, to be honest,' said Lucas. 'I'm just no good at playing it. I'm better at, y'know, arty stuff.'

'Your photo was the clear winner in the comp, Lucas,' said the AFL rep. 'It really stood out. Don't think the only way to be a part of footy is as a player. You could be the top sports photographer in the country one day.'

A massive grin spread across Lucas's face.

Then the Grand Final teams ran out onto the field.

Even Lucas jumped up and cheered. The roar of the crowd was deafening.

Nick remembered Hawthorn's Shaun Burgoyne being interviewed when he chalked up the most Grand Final appearances of any current AFL player. He'd said that it never got any easier, but that you've just got to enjoy the moment.

It was good advice.

Nick decided that nothing was going to stop him enjoying his moment. Not his disappointment at missing out on the captaincy. Not an argument with his friends. And not the space goop or Cactus's weird threats, either.

The Grand Final was a fierce contest from the word go. It was attacking footy at its best. Scores were locked at quarter time when the AFL rep led all the Crocs back down to the change rooms to begin warming up.

They watched the second quarter on TV screens. A whole stack of players were making premiership heroes of themselves. Would Nick be able to serve it up on the big stage too?

He eyed off his teammates. They'd been through so much this season. Yet again he was heading into battle with them.

And in no time, the siren sounded.

The Crocs were about to take the field.

# Chapter 6

**Ella led the Crocs up to the field. She** glanced back to ensure everyone was ready, then they all ran out.

Nick's stomach flipped as he crossed onto the hallowed turf, where all his heroes had run before him. It was pure adrenalin. He felt invincible.

Collingwood captain, Scott Pendlebury, said that when you hit the field on Grand Final Day you feel like you can run through a brick wall. And now, Nick totally understood what he meant.

The stadium looked different from the centre. There were faces everywhere, all blended together. Nick looked up at the 360 degrees of towering stands and felt minuscule. The actual playing area seemed enormous. He was glad the officials had marked out a smaller field for their exhibition match.

'Pretty cool,' said Ella as she ran past.

It was a serious understatement.

The Crocs got into their positions. They were playing a South Australian team — the Aldinga Sharks Under Elevens — in two five-minute halves.

Nick shot Bruiser a smile: the first in a while.

The junior ump whistled in the centre. She bounced the ball and they were away.

Bruiser won the tap.

'That's my boy!' called Mr Baxter on the boundary. Lucas and the Sharks' junior photographer stood with the official AFL photographers. Marz, Mr Blumfield and Mr Morris cheered from the stand.

Ava scooped up the footy and hand-balled to Ella who fought through traffic with the skill of Carlton's Bryce Gibbs.

Ella confidently stabbed it low to Nick. Clearly, she was cured of the nerves she used to get when her dad was watching.

Nick was too far out to score. There was a pack closer to goal, but no one could break free. He spotted Cam at the rear and kicked up over the group.

Cam dropped towards goal, then marked and slotted it straight through.

First goal to the Crocs! The crowd's applause filled the air.

'Awesome start!' yelled Ella. 'Jake, switch to the pocket. We need your speed up forward. Ava, great inside ball — keep it up! We can do this, Crocs.'

Nick thought so too. And Ella was the key. The way she utilised her players showed natural footy smarts and the team hung off her every word. They were playing *with* her, not *for* her. Something Taylor — and perhaps Nick — had never quite managed.

'Nice work...Captain,' he said.

Nick may have had his heart set on the captaincy, but he could see that Ella deserved it more than anyone.

She gave him a nod.

After that it was a low-scoring affair. However, both sides managed a goal before the five minutes was up and they swapped directions.

'Keep it up and this game's ours,' said Ella in the huddle. 'The game plan's working and we're really playing as a team.'

Nick grinned. 'We've got something special now,' he said. 'Something we didn't have at the start of the season. Something that doesn't come easy. We've got pride in the jumper. Can you feel it?'

Jake nodded. Cam puffed out his chest. Ava smiled. It had crept up on them, but they all knew it was true.

'You're right, Nick. Let's do this,' said Ella. 'Together, let's show the country that being a Croc really means something!'

The Crocs won the opening bounce in the second half, and Ollie booted it to the wing. It stayed up in the air long enough for Nick to spot the TV cameras in the stands.

The footage on the big screen was hard to ignore. Especially the replays of the Crocs' highlights, like Cam's first goal.

Watching the screen, Nick started to forget about his newfound pride in the

Crocs as a team. He became desperate to kick a goal. He couldn't go goalless when the whole footy world was watching! Today was his chance to be noticed.

The Crocs were 3 points down as Reevers booted the ball long from the centre.

Nick sprinted off his opponent to the pack that had formed underneath the ball. He came bolting through from the side, stuck both arms up into the air and ripped the ball out of the sky. It was just like former Swans' star Leo Barry, when he secured victory in the 2005 Grand Final.

Nick watched his screamer replayed on the big screen. The crowd cheered once again. This was his moment.

Bruiser was in his field of vision.

'Take the set shot!'

Mr Baxter's words from training echoed in Nick's head: 'Don't try to be flashy!'

But this is my chance, he thought. There are four million people watching on telly. One hundred thousand in the ground. If I play on, I could be a match-winning superstar. Surely there's enough time left on the clock!

He looked to Ella. She was shaking her head. He'd taken a similar mark in the dying moments of a game earlier in the season. Playing-on had cost the Crocs a victory.

No. He knew what he had to do.

He kept to his line, and started his run-up just as the ump whistled to signal the end of the game. Time was up.

'Great team footy, Nick,' called Ella.

'Bang it home for our second ever win!' called Mr Baxter.

Nick kept his head over the ball, picked out a banner behind the goals to aim at, and booted the footy.

It spun through the air. Dead on target.

'Nice kick!' Taylor blurted out.

The Crocs were going to win at the Grand Final!

Nick had both hands in the air, jogging backwards, set to erupt.

The footy dipped as it headed for the gap between the goals. Then it seemed to freeze in mid-air. Something had speared through it, stopping it dead.

'Huh?' said Nick, blinking a few times, certain he was seeing things.

The footy had been skewered by what looked like a long pointy branch.

'Hey, no fair! What's going on?' yelled Reevers.

The branch drew back out of the footy. The ball dropped, and Bruiser caught it just in front of the goals.

The Sharks started yelling and hugging, celebrating their victory, and the crowd cheered. But Nick ignored it all. His eyes followed the rest of the branch. It reached all the way up over the Great Southern Stand.

Ella and Bruiser ran to Nick. He turned to them. 'Cactus is here.'

Beyond the Great Southern Stand, tree branches writhed around like snakes.

'Raise the alarm,' said Nick. 'Cactus has control of the trees outside the stadium. There's no telling what he's got planned.'

'I reckon we're about to find out,' said Ella, pointing over Nick's shoulder.

Cactus came into view. He was high above the stand, surfing on a tree branch. And this time he was in full-blown weed-creature mode.

# Chapter 7

**As Cactus was lifted over the stand and** soared towards them, Nick realised he was even bigger and meaner than before. He had evolved. Into an uber-Cactus.

The MCG crowd fell silent, unsure what to make of it all. A few people applauded as if it was part of the half-time entertainment. The Crocs and the Sharks looked up, confused.

'Woah,' said Ella. 'He looks mega-freaky.'

'And scary-happy,' said Bruiser. 'Why is he smiling?'

'Hello, old friends!' cried Cactus as he hovered above them. 'I was hoping *weed* all meet again.'

'I didn't picture it like this!' cried Nick. 'Where've you been all year anyway?'

'Locked up in Mum's lab,' said Cactus. 'Not even she could find a cure for what I've got. I'm sick of being a science experiment, and being grounded is soooo boring. So I found a way out.'

The branch lowered Cactus to the ground.

'I get that,' said Nick. He tried to convince himself that maybe all Cactus wanted was to watch the big match.

'You get it, do you? I'm not sure you actually do get how it feels to be trapped,' said Cactus. He gestured with his vine-like hand. 'So, let me show you.'

Suddenly a patch of grass began growing directly below every player. Each growth thrust a different kid upwards.

'Woah!' Nick felt as though he'd left his stomach behind. He was at the top of something that looked like Jack's beanstalk from the old fairy tale. And the stalk was getting taller every second.

'Aaaaugh!' yelled Reevers as he rose.

'Put me down,' cried Ava.

The thick stalks grew till they were almost as tall as the grandstands. Nick felt the grass wrap around his chest. His stalk drooped at the top.

Some players were head first towards the ground, others feet first, but everyone

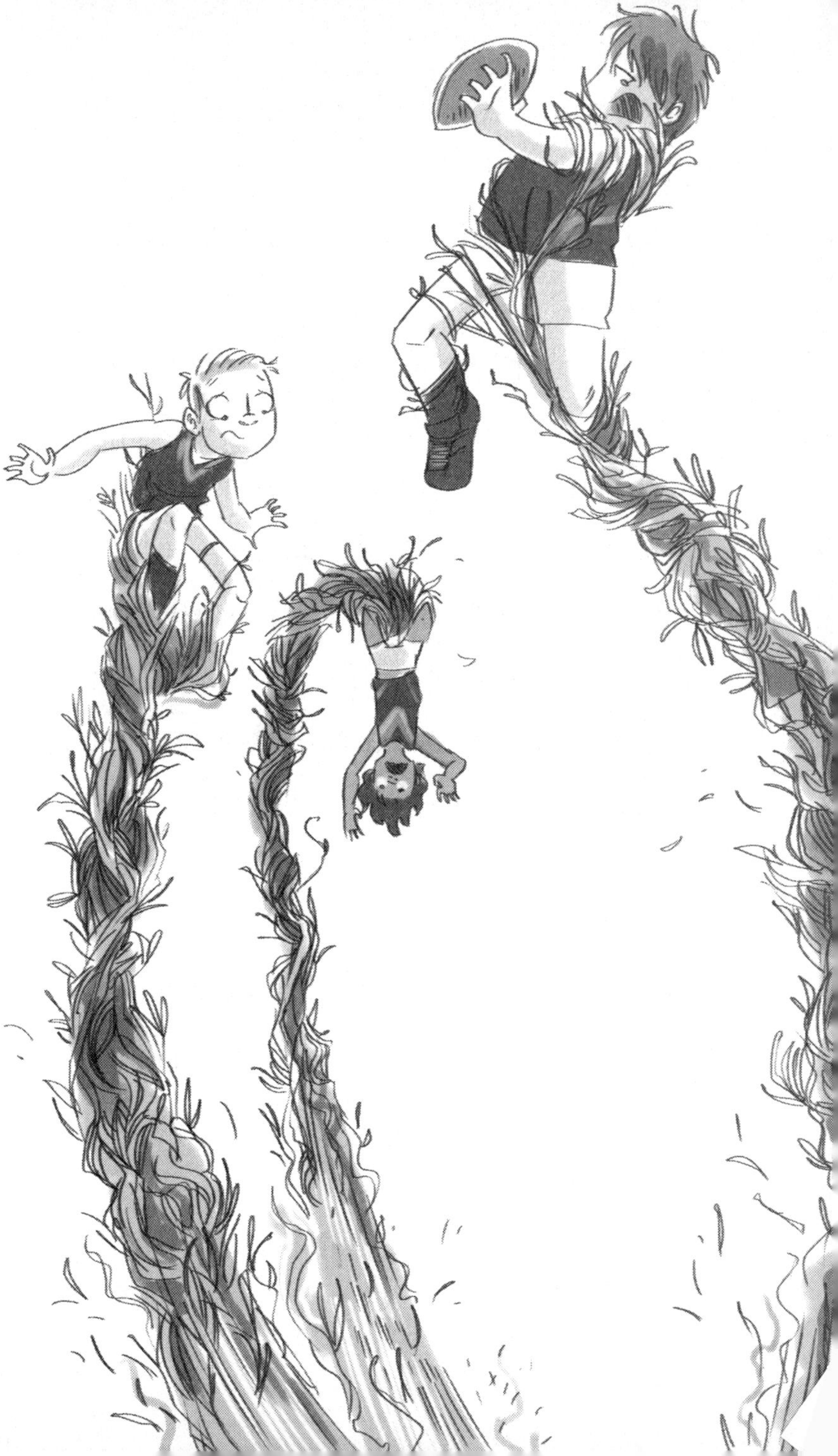

was tied up at the end of their giant stalk by lengths of grass.

Ella was squirming upside down on Nick's left.

Bruiser was suspended the right way up on Nick's right. He still held the punctured footy. 'This isn't how I pictured the game playing out,' he said.

Security guards and police were jumping the MCG fence. But with a flick of his wrist, Cactus created a grass barrier that stretched right around the boundary. The authorities began trying to force their way through.

Mr Blumfield and Mr Morris were dumbfounded up in the stands. Mr Morris was pointing at Cactus and shouting something.

Then Nick spotted what Cactus had in

his hand. It was the footy filled with space goop. It was fuming like crazy.

Despite being so high up, Nick tried to bust free. But the more he wriggled, the tighter the grass snaked around his chest. 'What are you doing with that?' he yelled at Cactus.

'Oh, this?' asked Cactus, shaking the footy, causing a fierce bubbling sound. 'Mum's files said this purple stuff's probably what caused me to start weeding out. She suspected it might cure me too, if she could track it down. But in the end I had to steal it personally,' said Cactus, tossing the ball to himself. 'Only to discover that it just makes me *more* weed!'

'Seriously. I'd be careful with that ball if I were you,' said Ella.

'So, I shouldn't do...this?' asked Cactus.

His vine-arm thrust the footy towards Ella. She gritted her teeth, but it sprung back to Cactus like a yo-yo.

'Stop it! You don't know what that substance is capable of,' said Nick.

'I have my suspicions,' said Cactus, continuing to hurl the space goop footy around Ella. 'And I reckon it'll be fun.'

The footy glowed so brightly that Nick had to look away. He noticed branches had grown up over all the stands' roofs. It seemed the stadium was enclosed by thick foliage.

Nick hacked at his stalk with his boot studs. He could feel it weakening.

'What are you up to there, Nick?' asked Cactus, spinning his way.

'Nothing,' said Nick, freezing.

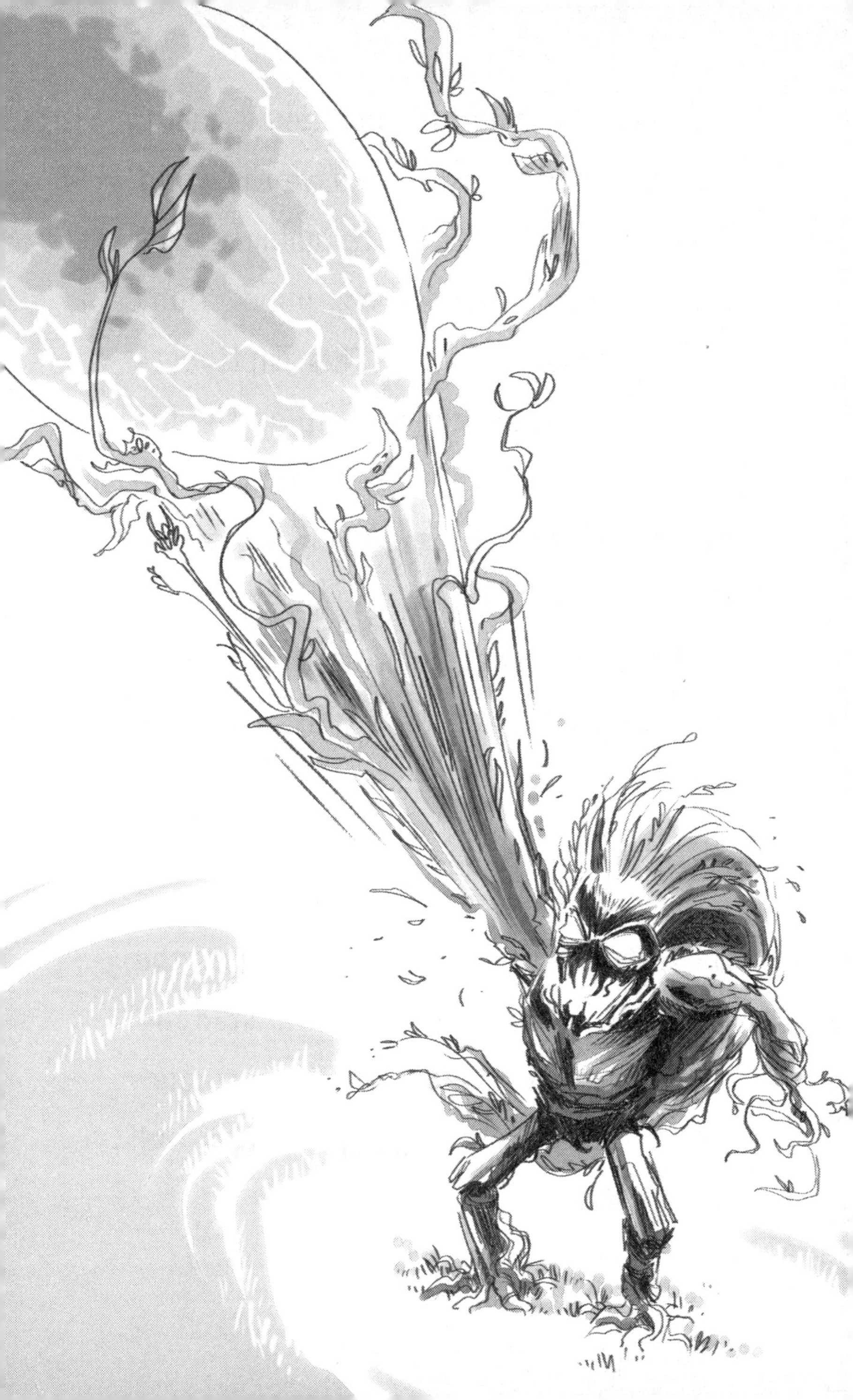

'Always playing the big hero.' Cactus laughed. 'Always trying to save the world.'

'Kyle!' A woman's voice boomed over the speakers around the ground. 'Don't do anything silly, dear. This isn't you.'

Mrs Cassidy's face came up on the big screen. Nick spotted her being filmed by one of the TV cameras in the crowd. Mr Morris was behind the camera.

'Nice to see you, Mum,' Cactus yelled as he sent out a branch to grab her waist. 'But you'd better get outta here. Cos things are about to get wild.'

'Please stop, Kyle!' she cried as the branch began to lift her over the Members' Stand and out of the stadium. 'The substance in that ball is unstable.'

'Duh. That's what I'm counting on!' said Cactus.

He swung the footy around furiously.

Nick flinched. 'Why are you doing this?'

'Well, since I can't be cured, Mum's company are sure to track me down and never let me out again. That's sooo not happening.'

'But —'

'But what, Nick? I'm a prisoner. Everything I care about has been taken away. Don't you think there'd be one or two things you'd miss if you were locked up?'

Nick thought about it. His friends? Sure. Party pies? Definitely. But he knew what he'd miss more than anything.

'Footy,' Nick replied.

Cactus nodded. 'Spot on. So, I figure, if I can't play football, no one can.' He laughed. 'I'm here to destroy footy forever!'

# Chapter 8

**Nick slashed his boot studs into the** grassy stalk, still hoping to weaken it.

Cactus was mesmerised by the space goop footy's fumes. Bubbles had started to form on its surface.

Nick caught Bruiser's eye. He nodded towards the purple footy, then to the punctured game footy in Bruiser's hand. The big guy gave a thumbs up. Nick hoped he understood.

Hacking into the stalk suddenly paid off — the whole thing drooped forwards and down. It was terrifying. The blades of grass around his waist split and he quickly reached around to hug the main stalk so he wouldn't fall.

He slid downwards, hitting the ground with a thump.

'I don't need to save the world, Cactus,' Nick yelled. 'I'll just settle for saving footy. Now, Bruiser! Kick!'

Bruiser dropped the game footy onto his boot and hoofed it.

The ball smacked the purple footy right out of Cactus's hand. Ever since the big fella had hit the queen bug, Nick didn't doubt his accuracy under pressure.

The space goop ball fell to the ground. It was pulsating. Clearly the footy wouldn't hold the goop for much longer. Nick picked it up. It was almost too hot to hold.

Somehow he had to get it out of the stadium.

But Cactus whipped out with his vine-arms. Nick jerked sideways to avoid them. They cracked like whips beside his head.

Cactus swiped one vine-arm sideways. Nick jumped it. And it sliced straight through Bruiser's and Ella's stalks. The grass collapsed.

'Ahhh!' screamed Bruiser and Ella as they tumbled downwards. All Nick could do was watch.

But the severed stalks fell in a heap and provided a soft landing. The piles of grass broke their falls.

Nick tried to pass Bruiser the footy,

but Cactus stomped, stabbing out a bolt of grass.

Thrown sideways, Nick handballed in mid-air.

Ella caught the ball and Cactus ran at her. He was furious.

With his focus on retrieving the ball, all the other stalks collapsed as well, lowering the rest of the players.

Cactus stomped again, sending blasts of grass at Ella. She swerved left and right to avoid them. Then she leapt over Cactus's vine-arms. Even Gary Ablett Jnr would've been impressed with her moves. But how was she going to escape? wondered Nick. Grass blocked off the boundary, plus the whole MCG had been overgrown!

Ella handpassed Bruiser the ball.

'Can you kick it out of the ground?' she asked.

Bruiser spun to face the Great Southern Stand. 'Cats' legend Bill Brownless once kicked a footy over a thirty-metre silo,' he said. 'The Great Southern Stand is forty-five metres high and I'm no Bill Brownless.'

'Less talk, more tonk!' Ella cried.

'You've gotta try,' called Nick.

But Bruiser didn't move. He just slowly turned to Cactus, who was sprinting towards him.

'Kyle,' he said. 'You can have the ball back.' He held it out.

'What?' said Nick.

Cactus seemed confused too. He paused, just as his vine-arms were about to swipe up the footy.

'Because I think your mum's right. I don't reckon you really want to do this. We know you. We know how much you love footy. And you're still the same person underneath.'

Then Ella turned to Cactus. 'Look, Kyle. I think you're a massive creep, an attention-seeking whinger, and you're dangerously reckless.'

'But?' said Cactus.

'But what?' said Ella.

'Um, come on, Ella. Cut him some slack. He's been locked up for months,' said Bruiser.

'I suppose it's normal to freak out a

little,' said Ella. But she didn't look like she completely meant it.

'Or a lot.' Nick glanced around at the grassy obstacles that littered the MCG surface. 'Look, Cactus. You can either choose to go down in history as the boy who destroyed footy. Or, with your powers, maybe you can choose to be the boy who saved it.'

'And if you do save it, and you can keep your powers under control, then you can play with the Crocs in our league,' said Bruiser. 'You've been playing an age level up, right? So you'd totally be allowed in our team next season.'

Cactus nodded, ever so slightly.

Then Ella started thinking like a captain. 'What team couldn't use an extra attacking midfielder? But you'd have to promise not to be such a jerk.'

Bruiser was juggling the searing hot space goop ball. The substance inside was boiling. It was about to force its way out of the footy. In the middle of the MCG.

'So, what do you reckon, Kyle?' Nick asked. 'Do *you* want to be the big hero this time?'

# Chapter 9

**The glowing ball started splitting at the** seams.

Cactus looked uncertain.

'C'mon,' said Ella. 'It's now or never.'

'You can do it, Kyle,' said Bruiser.

'Okay,' said Cactus. 'What do I do?'

Nick took the ball and booted it into the air. 'Send the grass up! Launch that footy right outta here!'

Cactus reached out — a pillar of grass

soared into the sky. It caught the ball, hurling it upwards.

Cactus grew the stalk taller and taller. Thick purple fumes were streaming behind the ball.

The footy burst.

*ShhhhwOOOOOMP!*

The space goop exploded and expanded into a massive purple sphere above the MCG.

Everyone ducked, covering their ears. If it had been at ground level it would have completely enclosed the stadium, but Cactus had got it even higher than the seagulls.

Then the sphere sucked itself inwards and disappeared in a puff of smoke.

The crowd roared.

Someone on the PA declared, 'What

a show! Best half-time entertainment ever!'

Nick and Ella got back onto their feet. Bruiser helped Cactus up. He looked like a human again — regular old spiky green-haired Kyle.

'Nice work,' said Ella. They looked around — the MCG was back to normal.

'Maybe there's no cure for what you have,' said Bruiser. 'But you can control it. The solution's the same as it's always been. You've just gotta keep your cool.'

'And there'll be no temper tantrums on my team,' said Ella.

Cactus nodded.

Ella, Bruiser and Nick directed the Crocs and Sharks off the field.

Mr Blumfield gave them two thumbs up from the stand.

'I guess our actions didn't reflect too badly on the school after all,' said Nick.

He glanced around at the Crocs. It suddenly hit home to Nick that this was what footy was truly about. Sure, awards and superstardom were nice. But being part of a team beat everything. No wonder Cactus had missed playing footy so much...

But before Nick left the field he still pulled a quick handstand.

On the bus, after the big game, Nick, Bruiser and Ella crowded around Lucas, looking at the shots he'd taken. The final image was of the Crocs with the confetti going off in the background as the Premiers held up the cup. What a day!

The minibus pulled up at school and their parents were waiting with a barbecue in front of the grandstand. Everyone piled off.

Nick waved at his mum, but Mr Morris held Nick, Ella and Bruiser back. He glanced out at the oval.

'It's been a remarkable season,' he said. 'And we wouldn't be here today without some heroic efforts from you three.'

'Thanks, Mr Morris,' said Nick.

'From now on,' he said, 'I think we're going to be a *happy team at Cobar.*'

Over by the barbecue, Nick interrupted Lucas telling their mum all about what had happened.

Their mum was beaming, but didn't look like she believed it.

'I'm so glad you both enjoyed it,' she said. 'I caught the start of your game on telly at work, but I missed all the special half-time entertainment you're talking about.' She hugged them hard.

'And I've got great news. I'm getting a promotion! No more late nights and weekend shifts for us,' she said. 'And just one job!'

'Don't tell Ella,' said Nick. 'She'll put

you straight on the parents' half-time oranges roster for next year.'

Before it was time to head home, Nick kicked off a rendition of the Crocs' theme song.

As everyone cheered at the end, Bruiser shook his head. 'Well, um, that was a day we won't forget.'

'Massive!' said Nick. 'It's a sleep-in for me tomorrow, for sure.'

'Guess again,' said Ella. 'Tomorrow we begin pre-season. I've got the whole thing planned.'

Nick believed in preparation as much as anyone, but he also believed in sleeping in, so he changed the subject. 'Lucas's photo of us at the MCG is going in the yearbook. Maybe the Harvster should offer Blumfield a few words to go with it to sum up the Crocs' awesome season.'

'Sure he'd want that?' Ella smirked.

'Um, how exactly *would* you sum it up?' asked Bruiser.

Nick cleared his throat, and got all serious. 'Something like, *Dear readers, footy, like life, has its ups and downs.*

*But if you give it your all, perform selfless acts of bravery, make a true hero of yourself —'*

Ella cut him off. 'You lost me at "dear readers".'

'Might be a bit long,' admitted Bruiser. 'How about: *Footy rocks!*'

Nick thought about it. 'Yep. Perfect, big fella. FOOTY ROCKS!'

# CRAWF'S FOOTY SKILLS

Here's a handy trick for passing to a teammate when there's no one providing an obvious lead. Nick used it perfectly to set up the Crocs' first goal at the Grand Final. It's basically an up-and-under kick that carries over a group of players, but it can be a very useful tactic.

> I use my trusty hula hoop as a target.

**2** Instead of kicking flat and hard, loop the ball over the top.

**3** And if you hit the target — always celebrate with some hula hooping!

## FROM THE AUTHORS...

What a way to end the Crocs' season! The team have developed out of sight since losing to the Panthers in Round One and we hope you've enjoyed the ups and downs of the Crocs' journey.

And maybe you can relate to the lessons Nick has learnt along the way. So that next time you come up against weed creatures, robots or mutant bugs, you'll know exactly what to do!

For more information on Kick it to Nick, fun downloads, or for pointers on how to improve your skills, head to crawf.com.au or kickittonick.com

**Crawf**  **Adrian**